HANNAH CLAIRE SMITH

HOW TO CONTROL THE WORLD

A Novella

ISBN: 979-8-9919598-0-3

Edited by Melissa Peitsch

Introduction to the Forces

Dear Allen,

I'm so pleased you reached out. Since your father passed, I've been hoping to hear from you and finally be given the opportunity to offer you what I believe is the greatest heirloom our family has ever possessed—a special knowledge. Things are quickly shifting in the world; to maintain our influence, these tools will prove more vital to your generation than they ever were in mine. But before I begin, there is something you must first understand and accept.

One can accumulate only so much power and wealth without the participation—or rather, manipulation—of the masses. Plenty of people are content with whatever they've accumulated honestly, but for some of us, it's not enough. For as long as I can remember, I simply cannot settle for what has been allotted to me by fate. My instincts tell me that you and I are alike in this regard, so I've given serious consideration to your request for advice. Our family has been cursed with a great hunger—but blessed with the knowledge, tools, and resources to satisfy it. Through our correspondence, I wish to equip you with these same abilities so that you, too, can possess everything you desire. If what I've shared is distasteful to you, then please discard this letter and feel no obligation to respond. But if this resonates, even in the slightest, then continue reading.

(Ensure these letters remain hidden from prying eyes. Our family's influence depends on the discretion with which this knowledge is passed. For your protection—and mine—destroy each letter after reading, or secure them carefully.)

I'm glad you're writing to me now, for I fear that, without effectively exploiting the tools at our disposal in the coming decade or two, you could lose the grip our family has spent centuries establishing. Whispers of change, of revolution, are carried on the wind from all four corners of the earth. The apathy we've carefully cultivated within societies everywhere is waning, and there is great potential on the horizon for something new, something that has never been seen before. Fighting this change may prove futile; guiding and directing it may become our goal. And if new methods and paths must emerge, ensure that—beneath the surface and beyond their idealism—they still house the necessary components for our manipulation. While the tools I'll share can and have been used at any and every moment in history, their cultivation and harnessing are more crucial than ever in times like these. Not only will I be your teacher, but the events of each day can also serve as your teacher. Observe, always, and if you have questions as things unfold, I am here to answer them.

There's a radical simplicity to the ideas I will share with you. They may strike you as obvious (perhaps too obvious), but I find that's the nature of life's most valuable and overlooked truths. These letters will transform you—let them. I'm giving you eyes to see, and you will never again view the world the same way once you understand one thing: the forces. The forces are primal. Unseen currents flow beneath the surface of human interactions. Few recognize the forces, but almost all are bound by them. Once you understand them, they become tools to command. When you wield them, you will become unstoppable.

These forces are the pillars that prop us up; they're the social currents and myths that inspire people to harm themselves, harm one another, or stand by as others are harmed. They are the energies you'll learn to harness to accumulate and maintain great power and wealth. Once you understand them, you'll see the forces slithering through people and society, possessing unaware minds. Regardless of your (or my) participation or engagement, you'll notice that these influences work toward the demise of those they infect. The tools I'll share with you can unlock the ability to become godlike. You'll discover that the forces await you to harness them. And where they aren't flourishing, they can be created and nurtured with the right tactics. Your ancestors and I have identified four forces so far, though there may be more we have not yet observed. They all operate similarly and seem to follow some natural law.

All forces can be neutralized by their opposite, and there is a particular resilience against all the forces we can cultivate.

The first force is **victimization**. It is a crucial instrument in wartime but can also flourish in times of peace. When there is a wound—someone is either physically or emotionally hurt, or something is unjustly taken from them—and there is a lack of adequate resolution, **victimization** takes root. When a person feels victimized, something prevents the wound from closing and healing. The obstructions allow this open wound to fester, and the individual begins to adopt the identity of a victim. This launches them into an unending power struggle between themselves and the world. They may oscillate between resignation to powerlessness or pursuing power over others, spreading **victimization** further like a virus. They can easily grow obsessed with retribution and get lost in fantasies of taking matters into their own hands. As long as they are under **victimization's** influence, they remain bound to those who hurt them and the traumatic event itself.

Sometimes, they'll remain in this state for months, weeks, years, or sometimes even an entire lifetime. Your aunt, my dear late wife, was afflicted by this force, sinking into a state of perpetual helplessness that I believe stemmed from some grave misfortunes in her early years. Despite being surrounded by our vast wealth and power, she never truly felt in control of her circumstances. **Victimization** is tragic when it possesses those we care about, but when it possesses those we seek to control, it creates significant opportunities. Whether a victim chooses to sink into helplessness or to take power over another, we can use them to our advantage.

The second force is **isolation**—a distinct absence of connection, whether physical, mental, or emotional. The need to belong is fundamental to our nature as humans. When this sense of belonging is absent, much like **victimization**, it often drives people down one of two distinct paths or causes them to oscillate between both. The first path is resignation—when one decides that the pursuit of connection is not worth it, causing them to withdraw into an empty life, void of connection. **Isolation** can also lure us down the second path—seeking out social groups that offer membership if (and only if) they meet certain conditions. These conditional requirements force adaptations of the self, the loss of authenticity, and the neglect of one's deeply held values. But just as revenge fails to satisfy the need to overcome **victimization**, conditional belonging also lacks the substance to satiate our desire for genuine connection. Yet, many will still pursue it.

I've wrestled with whether **isolation** should be considered a force. It feels more like an unmet need and a spark for desperation. After all, hunger, thirst, homelessness, and similar conditions aren't considered forces… so why should **isolation** be? I've accepted its significance above the other unmet needs for several reasons. It operates according to the forces' rules in that its opposite (belonging) is an infinite resource—unlike food, water, shelter, and so on.

Additionally, the root of this unmet need is contained within itself, whereas the forces often lie at the root of the other unmet needs. For instance, when someone lacks food, water, or other basic necessities that shouldn't be scarce in society, something else—usually some form of theft—is at play. In other words, justice—which is **victimization's** opposite—can alleviate much of the hunger, thirst, and homelessness in the world, but it cannot cure **isolation**. I'll explain further in future letters.

The third force is **fear**. **Fear** as a force causes people to choose whatever they perceive is necessary for immediate self-preservation or comfort over their commitment to their values. Like all forces, **fear** drives people toward hypocrisy. When **fear** takes hold, individuals may commit heinous acts or blindly follow brutal leaders. They'll do things the more secure versions of themselves would never dream of, leading either to shame or a profound forgetfulness of their individuality and their humanity. Things can quickly dissolve into anarchy when we fail to harness this force as it grips a population. When we can use **fear** to our advantage, there's very little that we can't convince people to do in the name of protecting themselves, their possessions, or their standing. After all, **fear**'s biggest lie is, "I didn't have any other choice." **Fear**, like all forces, does not need to be created by our hands for us to grasp and use it for our gain.

In these letters, I will not only discuss the forces and how to harness them but also how to avoid their influence. Some families and manipulators have learned to wield these forces to a degree but have also lived under their spell. This created significant limitations and hardships. You have heard in your youth of the tale of the mad despot, whose primary tool in maintaining his brutal regime was intimidation—but whose demise was triggered by his own delusions and paranoia. So be wary of **fear** and all the other forces, for they are convincing. And remember this maxim: whenever you feel you have no other choice, don't decide. Remain still until you discover the other options that are hidden from you.

Whenever you feel that you are being forced to do something, know there is no such thing as being truly controlled by someone. While others can control your body, only you can decide what you do with your mind. This secret lies at the root of your empowerment and resilience to the forces. Anchor yourself in this, and you will be far less vulnerable to the forces and, thus, to the manipulation of others. For every force, there are specific methods to build resilience and create immunity. Our goal is to always cultivate these qualities within ourselves while actively sabotaging their cultivation in society.

The fourth force is **ignorance**. This is perhaps the most apparent of all the forces, but it manifests in many forms, each requiring its own strategies for cultivation and management. We create **ignorance** either through manipulation or neglect. As the philosophers of old have taught us, it is not only necessary but also our responsibility to nurture a society that produces healthy, educated, responsible, and free individuals. So, if we stand in the way of that responsibility, we pave the way for **ignorance**. Neglect creates a lack of information, which creates fertile ground for manipulation through disinformation or misinformation and then fosters the **ignorance** required for our various endeavors.

As for the subtypes, here are a few to ponder, but I will explore each more thoroughly in future letters: There is the ignorance of self, which can be either shame, pride, or both. There can be an ignorance of the other, which can look like any sort of prejudice. There can be ignorance of present-day affairs, atrocities that are being committed, or what and who controls the world. This particular one grips the vast majority of people. There is also the ignorance of the past—how we teach what has occurred in our histories will shape what we believe is possible in the future. Many impossible dreams, after all, have already been realized before. We've simply managed to bury their evidence. The opposite of **ignorance** is education—the type that neutralizes **ignorance** at its deepest levels.

That concludes our brief introduction to those forces that allow us to harness the energy of a sick world. When and where the four forces are present, the people will be willing to sacrifice their autonomy for what they believe is necessary for self-preservation. But remember that tradeoff doesn't exist. Autonomy and self-preservation, in their truest sense, are inextricably linked. For if we sacrifice our autonomy in the name of saving ourselves, what is it we are exactly saving but a sort of partial self, an empty self? Secrets like these could lead to the demise of the manipulators' influence in the world. For this reason and others, always keep these letters and lessons private.

I'm anxiously awaiting your response,
Your Uncle

Channeling Political Opposition

Dear Allen,

Only two days after sending my last letter, I realized I hadn't addressed your most pressing question about the sparks of resistance against your companion's leadership, especially at what looks to be the dawn of a great war. There are two things I must express before I offer such wisdom.

First, I would prefer to offer you advice within the context of a deeper understanding of the forces, but I understand that this is an urgent matter. What you do—or fail to do—in the coming months could have significant consequences for your influence. Second, I am unaware of the lengths to which your father went in his instructions for maintaining the family's influence in the world. I am aware that you were never instructed on the role of these forces and how to harness them, but I was not aware that he failed to teach you what I consider a fundamental principle of our quiet rulership: separate the stage from the backstage.

We belong to a class of people I refer to as the manipulators. We are far from a secret society, as there are too many of us to count and little need or desire to create the interconnectedness necessary for such a club. Around the world, people like us quietly pull strings, reaping our rewards by exploiting harm. We have only one thing in common: much of our power and ease comes from maintaining an illusion. Think of the world as a theater. Most people are in the audience, unaware that the show they're watching is scripted. Politicians and celebrities are the actors on stage, basking in the attention and rewards of their roles, often forgetting that they're part of the act. We, however, are the producers—directing the narrative from the shadows. If the audience were to see us, the illusion would shatter. The power of the play is in its seamlessness, its invisibility.

All this is to say that maintaining a close relationship with someone whose job lies on the stage is dangerous. Private affiliation is necessary, but friendship? That level of connection can expose you. You must never allow affection or loyalty to cloud your judgment. In the end, your chosen leaders are tools. Nothing more. Be ready to discard them when the situation demands it.

Additionally, you must recognize that your only true opponents are those who threaten your influence, not those who threaten the influence of the leaders you support. The audience may boo and hiss at the actors on stage, but as long as they remain oblivious to the directors behind the curtain, our control remains unchallenged. Your most powerful opponents are both the forces themselves and those who want to eradicate them.

Keep this goal in mind always: never allow anyone to effectively neutralize the forces. It is better to see our leaders fall and swap them for new actors than to lose our influence through the eradication of the forces. If a great revolution does indeed come, remember that many such revolutions have come before. We have always remained committed to this goal and have been successful in achieving it.

When the monarchy fell two centuries ago, many manipulators believed their influence would also crumble. And many did. But those who were strategic retreated to the shadows, observed the emerging new world, discovered the vulnerabilities, and pinpointed where the forces could inevitably regain a foothold in society. Slowly, they planted seeds for their resurgence. Within a decade or two, the new systems (whose authors remained ignorant of the forces) led to ills, violence, and hierarchies similar to the old systems—just with different names, organizations, and faces. The forces are critical to your influence and all who, like us, seek more than their fair share; thus, your greatest risk is anyone discovering the forces' existence and pursuing effective methods for their eradication. That is why we must encourage successful revolutions to carry the illusion of real change while maintaining the myths and social currents that give us our authority.

The groups that wield control over others will shift; institutions, values, and governing systems will change; at times, the forces may become more subtle. But in everything we do, we must ensure that those forces persist. Without the forces, we cannot claim more than what is allotted to us by fate. We are reduced to the status of mortals or mere audience members—and I cannot imagine a greater agony. So even if someone intends to direct the violence inspired by the forces in a way that inconveniences you—perhaps someone is victimized and seeks revenge against those you've invested in and supported—those forces can still be of use to you. As long as they exist, even if they cause people to despise you or your leaders, they can be exploited.

Of course, the success of the uprising is not guaranteed. It is still in its earliest stages, so take heart. Let us now explore how to strategically quell rebellion and maintain your chosen leader's position. When it comes to rising political opposition, we use a layered approach to protect ourselves and our chosen leaders. Each line of defense serves a specific purpose, and if they become relevant to you, I will elaborate on them in future letters.

Our first line of defense is apathy—a shield to deflect opposition before it ever forms. While some have clearly freed themselves of apathy, many remain bound by it. We cultivate apathy in a variety of ways: We convince people that others' suffering is not their concern, that change is impossible, and that life's small pleasures are more important than fighting for something larger. We distract them with entertainment, indulgence, and noise—flooding their lives with trivialities so they never stop to think deeply about anything. By ensuring their comfort, even if only just enough, we create a society unwilling to risk losing what little they have for the uncertain promise of something better. Comfort, after all, is one of the most effective deterrents to rebellion.

When apathy fails—not just for the few but for the masses—our second line of defense is to lure them into inaction. We overwhelm them with complexity, bombarding them with information and opinions until they no longer know what to believe. At the same time, we attack hope directly, ensuring they believe that any attempt at change will be futile. We foster cynicism, convincing them that corruption is inevitable and that any effort to improve the system will only make things worse. This creates a paralysis, in which they are so bogged down by the immensity of the problem, that they never take the first step. It is essential here to sow distrust—not just in systems, but in their own ability to affect change.

If they begin to mobilize despite our efforts, we move to our third line of defense: isolating and dividing the movement. A movement that gains the passive or active support of the majority is dangerous, so we must prevent this from happening. Our task is to sever the connection between the movement and the general public. Discredit its movement's leaders, turn them into laughingstocks, or entangle them in scandals. Make their cause appear extreme, out of touch, or even dangerous. Without broad support, they become an isolated, fringe group, posing no real threat to our control. Divide them, pit factions against one another, and make them fight amongst themselves. Even better, let them accuse each other of betrayal or corruption. Once fragmented, they lose momentum and cease to be a force to be reckoned with.

Finally, if they cannot be discredited or isolated, our last resort is to turn the movement violent. If people must be radicalized, let them be radicalized in such a way that serves our interests regardless of the outcome. Often, movements will delude themselves into thinking that violence is distasteful but necessary to achieve some sort of utopian end, but they are wrong. Even if they succeed in overthrowing the existing powers, the cost will inevitably prove too high. In my experience, those victories achieved through violence carry violence—and thus, the forces—inescapably woven into their identity.

Additionally, the moment the opposition turns violent, your leader should be able to squash it easily. It's a game he is well-suited to play. After his crackdowns, he can create a narrative around the movement's immorality, proclaiming that his retaliation was necessary for the protection of the people and their most cherished principles. However, violent opposition carries inherent risks for your leader. A heavy-handed response could backfire, especially if it creates martyrs who energize the resistance. If your leader falters—misjudging available resources at hand or underestimating the passion of the opposition—it's wise to let the tides of change run their course, knowing the forces will persist, as the methods of revolution themselves created fertile soil. When the chaos subsides, we can return to reassert control.

Remember, it is not the fall of individual leaders that should concern you, but the awakening of the masses to the forces themselves. As long as they remain unaware, we can navigate any upheaval. And remember that while you need a certain level of resources and existing privilege to wield and harness the forces—and usually, even more, to create them on a mass scale—one does not need such things to neutralize them. This is why our knowledge, which I am sharing with you and which you will inevitably expand upon, must remain secure and out of reach of those who seek to liberate individuals and societies from our grip.

Regardless of one's social standing or economic resources, anyone can work to neutralize the forces. If the forces are exposed to enough people, and if those seeking to create something better persist in addressing them, we lose everything. That is why we must maintain the illusion of change without allowing true transformation. Let them believe they have a say and that their voices matter, while we continue to direct the narrative from behind the scenes. And always, always be sure to quickly snuff out any attempts to engage the forces. If the masses realize they are being controlled, their numbers—rather than our resources—will prevail.

With the weight of our legacy,
Your Uncle

Few Are Capable of Facing the Forces

Dear Allen,

I hope I didn't worry you too much with my last letter. I forget that this is all new to you, and I've never been particularly skilled at making the heavier truths palatable. Additionally, while numbers will inevitably win over resources if people awaken to the forces' existence and commit to their demise, don't spend too much time or energy worrying about that. Those who do identify the forces are usually unsuccessful at eradicating them for a few reasons.

First, many who discover them—like our family and other manipulators—are not exactly altruistic. When they see and taste the potential that comes with wielding these great instruments, they will be seduced, as their ancestors were before them. Their good intentions erode and even the few who remain pure are worn down by the forces, leading them to seek compromises or shortcuts—which ensures their failure. This will likely happen to leaders in emerging revolutions, as it has in many revolutions before. And the more one grows in influence, the more one's vulnerability to certain forces increases. Before they know it, they're on their way to becoming one of us.

Second, the few who discover the forces and want to improve the world often start on a small scale; as they seek to expand their ideas, the forces will find their way in as patience wanes and cooperation grows burdensome. As they attempt to scale their vision, collaboration becomes inevitable, but then egos rise. Soon, the self-aggrandizement so often needed for leadership transforms into self-destruction. Their lofty ideals crumble under the weight of their growing ambitions, consumed by the forces they once hoped to eradicate. There is no such thing as "the ends justify the means" when it comes to the forces. Preserving dignity for all is required to guard against the forces—which means honoring the humanity of even the least intelligent and most egregious among us—and that is an exceptionally trying task for most.

Third, those who seek to eradicate the forces within themselves, who understand how they operate and are able to cast aside their burdensome chains (if without the dangerous ambition), will often find themselves to be quite spiritual. Specifically, they will be drawn to those spiritual practices that cultivate disengagement from the world as an easier and more painless means of resisting the forces' influence. These individuals retreat into spiritual sanctuaries, removing themselves from the fray. Let them. Their detachment from worldly matters makes them irrelevant to our goals. They pose no threat to us, and sometimes it's better to let them enjoy their isolated peace than to coerce them back into the game. After all, they have not cultivated the strength necessary to face us or the forces on a systemic level; they remain nonthreatening to our ambitions.

Fourth, one of the fundamental rules of the forces is that as long as they exist, the world is less safe for everyone—except for those of us with considerable resources. One cannot selectively eradicate the forces, addressing harm in one area while ignoring harm in another. The forces are too deeply intertwined. Those who neglect this interconnectedness will find their victories temporary, as harm inevitably circles back to them.

And lastly, suppose a person cultivates immunity to the forces, stays morally pure, and can create the necessary strength and patience to endure and face those formidable forces en masse—not only for their own community but for communities everywhere. To rise above takes concerted effort, as I think you're beginning to see. The awareness and the self-analysis necessary to successfully become immune is an undertaking few choose—but these individuals do exist. When it comes time for them to educate the general population on the forces and how to free themselves from their grasp, this heroic individual will often find themself disappointed by the lackluster response of the people. When they try to teach the masses, they will be met with apathy. The forces provide a seductive comfort, shielding people from the weight of accountability. It is easier to remain asleep, cocooned in familiar illusions, than to face the raw truth. And so, the heroic individual stands alone, disillusioned by a populace that prefers ignorance over freedom. A simple external enemy, an individual or group, is far more appealing than one that also lies internally.

There is one exception to this: if there is a large enough group within the dangerous combination of present discomfort and the belief in a better future, mobilization is possible. With these two things, they may be both willing to take a chance to eradicate the forces and face the persistent discomfort that comes with the commitment to eliminate them internally and externally.

But again, these circumstances are rare.

In future letters, we will explore **ignorance** along with the types of education that we should allow and the types we should seek to eradicate. But I want to touch briefly on the most important type now, which we should commit to stifling to avoid the risk of the aforementioned mass awakening and mobilization: hope. Hope is the most dangerous truth. It is the seed that grows into revolution. Hope is learned; it is knowledge that something better is possible. It's different from naivety in that it is grounded in reality, even if it also exists within the imagination. Where there is discomfort, we must ensure that hope does not take root, for once people believe that something better is possible, they become ungovernable. Our task is to suffocate that hope, to cloud their vision, and make dreams of freedom impossible.

So, in everything you do, diminish hope.

Yours in confidence,
Uncle

Letter IV

Victimization

Dear Allen,

We are now one month into your first major war, making this the perfect time to analyze our first force and its many uses. Over the seven-odd decades of my life, I've witnessed many wars, and I've never seen a warmonger fail to harness **victimization** to his advantage. There is no military invention or innovation that can surpass the value of one's ability to wield this force.

War is a messy thing, but for those of us who want more than our share, it is a fertile ground for exploitation. Few truly benefit from war besides us, but the masses are easily convinced of its necessity through **victimization**. These benefits extend far beyond simple land grabs. Because we have many allies across political affiliations and industries, war's potential for profit and the expansion of our power is significant. From the sale of arms and equipment to the rise of nationalism (which consolidates control) to the people's reliance on their ultimate guardians—our appointed leaders—the rewards are numerous. Another secret of war is that the vast majority are tragically unnecessary to achieve whatever the public perceives as the intended purpose. Yet, we persuade them otherwise through **victimization**, often bolstered by other forces.

This reminds me: there is rarely only one force at play when harm is committed. **Victimization** seldom acts alone; there's almost always overlap, a synchronous dance amongst forces. More often than not, **victimization** joins hands with **fear**, **isolation**, and **ignorance**. Together, they reinforce each other, amplifying their potency. When one appears, the others are never far behind, and the manipulators' power grows exponentially.

Now, what exactly is **victimization**? **Victimization**'s goal is to convince you that you are powerless—either you can't do anything about it, or you must take power from someone else to regain your power. The former creates compliance, and the latter creates cycles of violence (violence begets more violence), both of which we can use.

To review, **victimization** is a force created when someone is harmed (physically or emotionally) or when something is wrongly taken from them with no resolution. The wound stays open, festers, and deepens. Where there is harm, we must make the most of it, either overtly or covertly standing in the way of resolution. There are a few types of **victimization** worth noting. The first is personal **victimization**, which occurs when we are harmed directly. The second is secondary or narrative **victimization**, which is when someone harms a group we identify with—be it our religion, tribe, or nation—and we take it personally. When no resolution follows, we, too, feel the sting of that harm. Regardless of who created the **victimization**, you can harness it to your advantage.

There is also false **victimization**, which is distinct from genuine **victimization**. False **victimization** is rooted in **ignorance** and thrives on fabricated grievances. There are two types of false **victimization**. The first arises when someone loses privileges they were never entitled to, such as when equality removes an unfair advantage. The second occurs when a narrative of harm is essentially made up—when people are told they've been wronged, even though the harm never occurred. Both types fuel resentment and are ripe for manipulation.

While the forces usually share a point of origin—**victimization** arises from unresolved harm, for instance—there are many ways to perpetuate and harness them. And there are two ways to neutralize them: embracing the force's opposite (an external method) and the cultivation of resilience (an internal method). **Victimization's** opposite is justice—but justice doesn't necessarily entail incarceration or punishment. True justice restores the broken humanity of both the victim and the perpetrator, addresses the root causes of the harm, and rebalances the scales. For example, if a neighbor steals your valuables, the true resolution would involve an apology, the return of the valuables, and addressing the desperation that drove the theft in the first place. This kind of resolution heals both sides and closes the wound.

True justice is rare and feared by manipulators like us. It doesn't merely punish; it restores dignity to both victim and perpetrator and addresses the circumstances that led to the injustice. That's why true justice is so dangerous—it breaks the cycles of violence and exploitation we rely on. False justice, on the other hand, is much easier to achieve and far more useful to us. It perpetuates **victimization** by offering superficial resolutions that never address the deeper harm. (Few have discovered the keys to satisfactory justice, however, so this should be no problem for you.)

Now that we know how **victimization** is created and perpetuated, let's explore how to harness it. When there is collective **victimization**, people will be easily tempted into supporting acts of revenge or domination. When someone feels powerless, they can so easily fall prey to the illusion that taking power from someone else will restore their own power. That's what makes retribution as seductive as it is unsatisfying. Harnessing **victimization** is one of the most effective tools to gain popular support for any war or act of violence. There's no greater hunger than the hunger to reclaim one's power. If someone chooses hopelessness instead, that form of **victimization** is equally useful. A hopeless victim will almost always obey—after all, what's the point of resisting when you believe you have no control?

Victimization also promotes mass disunity—or, in some cases, false unity. Unity built on shared grievances rather than shared values is fragile. I'll explain more about this when we discuss **isolation** and its companion, false belonging.

Now, if there is no justice, are those who've been harmed doomed to **victimization**? Not necessarily; this is when the internal method of eradication comes into play. There is a way for individuals to resolve harm on their own, and it's crucial for you to understand how to prevent this resilience from developing. Resilience is built when a person awakens to their own power and takes control of their healing, putting the harm in the past. They break free of the victim identity, though they may still pursue external justice.

One of the most important principles for you to understand, as a means of building resilience to **victimization**, is that harm is not personal. When we perceive harm as personal, we get caught up in questions of whether we deserved it, but this contemplation is neither helpful nor productive. Even when the perpetrator claims it is personal, the reality is that harm flows through society like molten streams; sometimes, to our own detriment, those streams find their way to us. Understanding this can help individuals move forward, allow their wounds to close and begin healing.

Obviously, for our societal approach, we must cultivate the opposite of what we foster within ourselves. In my next letter, I'll explain how to do just that—to keep individual and collective wounds open and festering, primed for our manipulation.

With care,
Your Uncle

Letter V

Creating the Ideal Environment for Victimization

Dear Allen,

In your last letter, you asked a good question: "What place, if any, should philanthropy have in our lives, especially in the context of harnessing and perpetuating the forces?" The answer is a significant one. Charities can play a critical role in perpetuating the forces and dissuading altruists from discovering and neutralizing them. This brings me to the topic of this letter: how to create an environment ripe for **victimization**.

The good thing about this task is that it's rather easy. The world we've crafted is already ripe for **victimization**, and to counter that is to swim upstream. Most simply don't have the strength to brave the currents. In the event that some cultural shifts occur after my passing, it's critical that you understand why the environment we've built is so primed for **victimization** and for the other forces to thrive.

Let's return to philanthropy. When someone has experienced **victimization**, they've experienced powerlessness. A charity interested in neutralizing the sense of victimization that follows harm will focus on re-empowering these individuals—we, in an effort to maintain the force's grip, must do the opposite. Philanthropy that fosters dependence, elevates do-gooders to hero status, or treats those they serve as broken and helpless, effectively keeps the "beneficiaries" in a state of victimhood. Thankfully, this is the norm today. It not only perpetuates the force; it strengthens it. Handouts, sympathy, and especially pity (my favorite) all play a role in crafting the right environment for this power. Pity is perhaps the most insidious tool. It disguises itself as compassion while reinforcing the victim's powerlessness. When we offer pity, we strip away their agency and keep them shackled to their victimhood, all under the guise of helping.

By generously funding these types of endeavors and rewarding charities that emphasize temporary solutions, we discourage more effective or sustainable projects. Those efforts, after all, will go unfunded and unnoticed.

You also asked how to know what type of justice to pursue and what systems should be created to address cases of harm. The system we have now is perfect as it is, and we must avoid any alterations that make it more victim- or perpetrator-friendly. To make the most of harm, both the victim and perpetrator should see a degradation of their humanity in the pursuit of justice. True justice restores humanity to both victim and perpetrator. False justice, on the other hand, either reduces the perpetrator to their worst acts or absolves them completely, ensuring the victim remains bound to their harm. It matters less if the punishment is too harsh or too lenient; it matters more that it causes both the victim and the perpetrator to remain in a state of unresolved violation.

Forgiveness, in its true form, is one of the most potent recovery tools for those who've been victimized. It releases the victim from their bond to the perpetrator and the incident itself. However, shallow forgiveness—the kind that is promoted too soon or without meaningful resolution— keeps the victim hostage to their pain. False forgiveness is an especially powerful tool. By encouraging victims to "let go" without offering real resolution, we keep them trapped in their pain. This type of forgiveness protects the perpetrator, isolates the victim, and ensures the community's comfort, all while leaving the door open for future **victimization**. So when proposing forgiveness, propose the type that leaves people feeling forced into it—void of justice and designed to undermine the healing of both the victim and perpetrator.

Just as we can undermine true forgiveness and justice with their superficial counterparts, we can do the same with peace. To create a false sense of peace—what we can easily label as 'order'—we divert attention away from real peacebuilding efforts by painting the voices of the oppressed and those fighting for change as threats to the comfort of the majority. By convincing regular citizens that any disruption to the status quo is intolerable or even dangerous, we ensure that the masses will turn against those advocating for meaningful change. This cultivates an atmosphere of blame, where the oppressed are cast as the agitators. In doing so, we prevent true peace from taking root while simultaneously maintaining the illusion that our chosen leaders are lovers of and advocates for peace—just as they appear to be for justice, charity, and forgiveness.

Another way to foster a community that ignores harm and fails to support its victims is by setting an unattainable standard for those deemed worthy of protection. This must be done subtly, tapping into people's desire for self-righteousness and their resistance to self-reflection. By perpetuating myths about how victims "invite" harm through their actions or behaviors, we create an environment where the responsibility for suffering is shifted onto the victim. The criteria for deserving protection become so rigid that most victims internalize their pain, convincing themselves they brought it upon themselves and retreat into silence and shame. This isolation keeps them voiceless, allowing perpetrators to continue their harm unchecked and perpetuating the power of **victimization**.

This strategy thrives when we've also cultivated an intense discomfort with vulnerability and pain. The illusion of safety must be so powerful, yet fragile, that no one wants to let another's suffering disrupt it. People will turn a blind eye to the injustice within their own communities in order to preserve their own comfort. Many buy into the idea that some people are inherently deserving of harm, because it allows them to believe they are safer than they truly are—that they can control their own environment, that harm won't come to them, and that there's no need to address the deeper, systemic roots of violence affecting the "imperfect victims" in their community. These myths and beliefs can go a long way, but there will always be a few who manage to forgive, heal, or free themselves from the grip of victimhood. These individuals are rare, but they do exist. In such cases, the only viable strategy is to limit their influence.

Now that I've explained how to maintain **victimization** within individuals, I must also share a vital tip on how we can keep **victimization** alive after a collective tragedy or trauma. To do so effectively, we must capitalize on every disaster through strategic storytelling. When we tell the story, we must make it seem as though the harm is still ongoing—that it could happen again at any time. The belief that harm is likely to be repeated keeps the wound open, preventing healing. Memorials should not only serve as places of remembrance but also as breeding grounds for revenge fantasies and hero narratives. By keeping the past alive in this way, we ensure that the pain lingers and the desire for retribution festers.

I once heard of a dictator who garnered support for mass atrocities by regularly referencing the violence his people had suffered under an empire more than a century prior. The group targeted for the atrocities had little to do with the original harm, but the dictator successfully channeled the old wounds into new violence. The art of victimizing history is one you should cultivate. We can direct the thirst for revenge toward any group—regardless of whether they were the original perpetrators. Any convenient scapegoat will do. As long as the wound remains, the masses will follow.

Yours,
Uncle

Letter VI

Isolation

Dear Allen,

I am writing to you from my summer retreat house, and I am here alone for the next month. The irony of me writing to you about the power of **isolation** is not lost on me. Perhaps this is the force I struggle with the most. Usually, I'm able to revel in my solitude. I savor those moments alone, but sometimes—and I think this is true for many of us manipulators—spending one's life in the pursuit of gross accumulation can prove lonely. When the majority of people have become mere tools to us, it becomes difficult to see the potential for friendship or intimacy.

And then, of course, there is the issue of vulnerability, which is necessary for connection but often impractical for those in our position. Vulnerability can be a bridge out of loneliness, but for us manipulators, it is a double-edged sword. The moment we allow ourselves to be vulnerable, we risk exposure—and in our world, exposure can be fatal. It is better to wield vulnerability as a weapon against others rather than opening ourselves to it. So, for the sake of protection, we allow **isolation** to creep in. But even in writing to you and sharing this small glimpse of vulnerability on this page, I have found some connection. I thank you for that. Our exchanges are providing both the intellectual stimulation and connection these mundane days often lack, renewing my purpose through this connection.

Isolation works much like **victimization** in weakening individuals by separating them from the strength found in unity. When isolated, people are more easily controlled, less likely to resist, and more prone to anxiety. Together, these forces create an environment ripe for manipulation. My description of **isolation** will be somewhat shorter than that of other forces, as its harnessing is more straightforward, requiring fewer strategies or recipes.

Isolation has been used since the dawn of conquest as a tool for control. Division is essential when ruling an unwilling party. Like all forces, **isolation**'s vulnerability to manipulation is its most advantageous quality. The goal when harnessing **isolation**, as with any of the forces, is to encourage people to rely on their "instincts" rather than their values or reason. These so-called instincts often lead them astray, working against their long-term well-being.

There are two types of **isolation**: physical and mental. These almost always interplay, as it is difficult to be physically isolated without feeling mentally isolated. Physical **isolation** is fostered by the way we structure society—homes and communities spaced far apart, making connection difficult. The greater the barrier to connection, the less people will seek it. Mental **isolation**, however, is required to truly wield the power of **isolation**. This is when individuals mentally distance themselves from others, whether by choice or circumstance. Mental **isolation** is the feeling of loneliness even when surrounded by others. Without real connection—without vulnerability—they experience a sense of emptiness in their social interactions.

Like those affected by **victimization**, the isolated person faces two choices: they can either give up on connection or fall into false belonging. In the former instance, they are more easily ruled because they are weakened by their disunity. As they grow more anxious in their **isolation**, they see innocuous things as threats and become more unwilling to take social risks. The illusion of self-reliance weakens them, making them vulnerable to manipulation. Once people believe they can do everything alone, they become nearly powerless against our resources. Remember, unity and numbers will always prevail if people awaken to the forces. The more isolated people become, the less likely they are to unite.

In the latter option, they are more easily controlled because you can offer something they desire—a sense of community—and they will do almost anything to obtain it. We can control most isolated people by dangling the promise of connection just out of reach. Offer them the idea of a utopian community, but make it conditional. The community must require conformity; the individual must sacrifice parts of themselves to fit in. False belonging is a powerful tool—people will do anything to escape **isolation**, even if it means giving up their true selves. Always ensure that this false unity is built on shared grievances rather than shared goals. This enhances **victimization** and the other forces.

False belonging can also be easily accessed through alcohol or other intoxicants. These substances create the illusion of connection, numbing the mind and dulling the need for real intimacy. Despite the common myth that one becomes more authentic under the influence, substances actually drown out the quiet, honest voice within. Shallow social interactions become more bearable, but the deeper desires for connection remain unmet. This is why bars, rather than coffee houses or tea shops, are historically favored by manipulators. They foster shallow connections and numb the mind, hindering true intimacy.

What sparks **isolation** in the first place? Anything that encourages or forces disconnection can create it. Luckily, we've already crafted the ideal environment. We've fostered a strong love of privacy—convincing people that the ideal home is one isolated from others, making connection more difficult. We've made one's job or career central to life and identity, ensuring that most workplaces are emotionally and intellectually exhausting, leaving little energy for social engagement. Additionally, we've witnessed a rise in the general distrust of outsiders, an erosion of social fabrics, and an overwhelming belief that one can do everything alone.

Pseudo-connections—like those found in bars, religious institutions, or militias—are thriving and providing shallow alternatives for those who fear vulnerability. They're offering the appearance of community, but the connections are thin and based on conformity rather than authenticity. Few people are truly known by others these days, and that is exactly how we like it.

Your mission is to protect and sustain what already exists rather than focusing on promoting **isolation**. The environment we've built already fosters it well.

As for you, to build resilience to **isolation**, prioritize quality over quantity in relationships. Real connection requires vulnerability, and you must be willing to show the parts of yourself you fear may be unworthy. Only through genuine connection can you neutralize the force of **isolation** from within. Opening yourself to true relationships with the right people is a must, and remember: while you may not need others for material needs, you need them for fulfillment.

If you have any thoughts to add, I'm eager to hear them.

Until next time,
Your Uncle

The Thing You Can Never Lose

Dear Allen,

I often wonder why your father didn't teach you these things before he passed. Perhaps he fell into the all-too-common trap of thinking he would be around forever. In all things, we must remain grounded in our own mortality. Your grandfather understood this well and made a point of instructing your father and me in the ways of the forces from the time we were just beginning to understand the world. While I do think it was a bit too early, as it drained much of our wonder, his commitment paid off in the end. Your grandfather possessed a firm understanding and respect for his mortality, whereas your father embraced notions of invincibility. Remember that these delusions are a type of **ignorance**, and we must work to remain immune.

I don't feel it's my place to assess whether the forces had taken hold of your father; I'm saddened to admit that we had very little communication after an argument nearly a decade ago. We disagreed on these very methods of control that I now share with you, which have been faithfully passed down for at least seven generations. I suppose intellectual hubris got the best of him—which is why I am grateful to have you as my pupil, with your heart and mind open to the methods of leadership that will be most advantageous for you, for me, and for the continuation of our lines and aims.

We cannot, as your father so earnestly tried to convince me, "leave behind our hunger for the search for true freedom." To abandon that hunger is to embrace a dangerous **ignorance**—a failure to see that true freedom lies not in renouncing our desires, but in mastering the forces that govern the world. We are like beasts, and ignoring our nature only brings suffering. Let us not pretend that our ability to thrive does not depend on the accumulation of wealth and power, which, by necessity, requires the suffering of some.

Always know what you possess, what can be taken from you, and what can never be taken from you. This knowledge—the understanding of the forces and how to manipulate them—is the treasure that no one can steal. It is the root of our power, passed down through generations, and with it, we have remained untouched by revolutions and coups. Your father's rejection of this knowledge was a form of **ignorance**, and we must remain immune to such delusions.

There are so many things the academics claim should be taken from the ruling class to equalize the population. Still, they—in their stuffy libraries and piles of books—forget to consider what is of most significant value to us. They can steal your wealth, your properties, and your positions, but they can never take the greatest privilege that being in this family affords you—the knowledge of how the world works and how to harness its energies to your advantage. With this knowledge, you could be left with nothing but your bare hands in a wasteland and still find a way to rise again.

The manipulators (and the super-rich and -powerful) never share the wisdom that allows us to navigate financial, political, and social systems more effectively than those not born to our types of families. Remember, that is your greatest inheritance. And with that, you have nothing to fear. We can always recover and rise again.

In trust,
Your Uncle

Do Not Fall Prey to the Forces

Dear Allen,

This will be another shorter letter, but I found myself somewhat concerned by your last correspondence. I fear your perspective on the rising opposition is steeped in the idea that these offenses you face are personal. You are allowing **victimization** to take hold, so I will share again what I think is the most valuable aspect of learning about the forces. As we have discussed in earlier letters, the forces are tools to be harnessed, but you must never allow them to take hold of your own life. The ability to manipulate the forces without being consumed by them is the key to true mastery.

Remember that it is a challenging but necessary task to work with the forces, to harness and partner with them, but also to deny them any influence in your own life. The only true freedom in this world is freedom from the forces. The forces will have a constant allure, and it only takes a moment of weakness for them to attach themselves to you, for them to infect your mind. You will become their slave—and perhaps worse, you will become the slave of others who know how to wield them.

This does not mean you must be free of vice. Do not equate "vices" with the forces. Certainly, a good number of vices are tied to the forces, but not all. For instance, the one I possess most passionately and proudly, greed, is not necessarily a force. Greed is not inherently a force unless you begin to feel entitled to what you desire or believe that you are owed something. It is when vices are linked to the forces—such as **victimization**, entitlement, or **fear**—that they become dangerous. I possess greed simply out of want; not because I think I'm better than anyone else, but because I see the level of wealth and power possible. I can feel it at my fingertips. Who am I not to grasp and take it?

I've been blessed with the intelligence and privilege necessary to expand my power beyond what any regular person could, and I'm determined to utilize the tools I've been given. Keep in mind, as I explore the various forces, that it will be advantageous for you to continue to explore your innermost self for their presence. The more you manipulate the forces, the greater your resistance to them must grow. The moment you begin to feel that something is owed to you—whether it's wealth, connection, or power—you open yourself to the influence of the forces. Entitlement is a gateway to **victimization**. Anchor yourself in the knowledge that nothing is truly yours, and you will find freedom from these traps.

Additionally, it is vital that only you remain free from the forces. It is not to your advantage that others, even those you might see as peers, are free from the forces. If others discover your freedom, they will become envious and seek the same, threatening your advantage. Keep this knowledge hidden, except perhaps from one trusted person—a partner who can challenge you to stay vigilant. We all have blind spots and need someone to reflect what we cannot see. But even then, be cautious of the **isolation** this knowledge may bring.

The forces will always seek to draw you in. Stay vigilant, for it only takes a moment of weakness for them to take hold. Freedom from the forces is your greatest weapon—guard it carefully.

Yours truly,
Uncle

Fear

Dear Allen,

Where there is **fear**, there is control. **Fear** is one of the most effective tools to persuade people to surrender control without conscious effort. As with **victimization** and **isolation**, **fear** is a tool that allows us to control people by convincing them to relinquish their autonomy. When I speak of **fear** as a force, I'm specifically speaking about the fear of harm, fear of **victimization**, and fear of loss. **Fear** can be used to inspire two things: obedience or reliance.

To foster obedience, we intimidate people into compliance. To intimidate the few, we can use a variety of measures, including personal threats and blackmail. Find the thing that someone is unwilling to live without, such as their reputation, and exploit it. For the masses, we can use either overt or covert means. For overt intimidation, selective force and threats can persuade the people to relinquish control and silence their voices. While brutish, this method can be useful when more subtle manipulations have failed.

To foster reliance, we harness and amplify the **fear** of some grave and impending danger to convince the populace to hand over some (if not most) of their autonomy. When used correctly, **fear** causes people to pay more in taxes, support unjust wars, and even engage in preemptive violence—actions they would never have considered under normal circumstances. They'll also submit to sacrificing their rights and privacy and accept the detention or torture of innocents in the name of security. **Fear** convinces people to sacrifice their freedoms and values in exchange for security that will never last. Our role is to offer that false sense of security—one that is temporary and demands a great price—before anyone can offer true safety. Security amid autonomy and integrity is dangerous to us, so we must ensure it never appears as an option.

This is most effectively done following a personal or collective disaster. **Fear** causes a regression that convinces people to see you, their leader, as a parent. They will follow you blindly, like children. This is why I never let a destructive incident pass without enhancing my power and encouraging the relinquishment of individual autonomy. This is the quick and easy path to a faux-security that so many, gripped by their nightmares, will heartily accept.

There is a healthy form of fear that drives necessary action for self-preservation, such as storing food in anticipation of a storm. Healthy fear drives us to protect ourselves and our loved ones. This is simply prudence, not a force. But the **fear** that turns into a force has a different quality—it overpowers the mind, blurs vision, and dissolves logic. The goal of **fear**, when we wield it as one of the four forces, is to convince someone to choose what they perceive as necessary for survival over their most deeply held values. Healthy fear is grounded in reality; it keeps us safe and prompts positive action. The **fear** as a force clouds judgment and persuades people to act against their long-term interests, and that leads to easy manipulation and exploitation.

The antidote to **fear** is safety and security. This is hopefully obvious to you. When someone feels safe, they do not feel afraid. But what builds that feeling of safety? It could be knowing that one is not alone, knowing that the threat is not as vicious as presumed; it can involve protective measures or knowing that there's a contingency plan if something happens. It might be simply understanding the true nature of the threat, dispelling fear of the unknown.

To prevent the establishment of security when we're seeking control through **fear**, especially in our more overt pursuits, we must ensure that people are unaware of their power and numbers. **Ignorance** and **fear** play well together. When people feel alone in their outrage, they are less likely to act. There is a tipping point in any resistance, when enough people join and enough security is established, that causes others who were silent to suddenly rush in. When this happens, you've already lost. Courage is not only contagious; it fosters security; it leads to increased action because it shows the powers of resistance and that others are willing to face its threat.

The **fear** of the unknown is especially powerful. If I tell a dissident they will be imprisoned and detail their treatment, it is less persuasive than if they simply know they'll disappear, with no other information but chilling uncertainty. When people don't know the extent of the threat they face, their imagination fills in the gaps, often making the **fear** worse than the reality. Preserve this uncertainty whenever possible—it is far more persuasive than the known.

You might wonder why courage isn't the antidote to **fear**, so let me explain. Courage and **fear** can coexist—you can be terrified of what you're facing and still stand up to it. Courage is resilience to **fear**, but safety is what neutralizes it. Security and **fear** cannot coexist. Courage is the individual's resilience to **fear**—a willingness to act despite **fear**, grounded in the knowledge that something greater is at stake.

Once, I had the opportunity to speak with one of our more formidable dissidents. She had courage in abundance, and I was curious about how she cultivated it. She was willing to sacrifice everything—her life, safety, and comfort—all for the ideal that her people could be liberated from the systems I helped to establish. It would be easy for me to see her as a foe, but there was something about her I was determined to learn from. She had something I wanted—freedom from **fear**.

We locked her away in a reeducation camp, but I visited her weekly. In our cold, dimly lit meetings, her dark brown eyes shone with determination. She was impossible to convince to betray her values. She saw that—even in chains—she was freer than I was, and she made no secret of how she achieved this freedom.

Courage, for her, combined three things: the ability to imagine a better future if she acted, the ability to imagine a worse future if she didn't, and the willingness to face discomfort in pursuit of her ideals. Many of us refuse to accept our power to create something better, clinging to false realism. Others fail to see how the slow erosion of autonomy will worsen their conditions in the future. She held both truths with an unwavering resolve, willing to face potential horrors to prevent a future worse than the present. It was something I had yet to fully cultivate.

These characteristics seem to be waning in each generation, which gives me hope. Courage is a dying breed. Create a society with both a lack of imagination and a low tolerance for discomfort, and you will find that it produces very few courageous individuals.

Until next time,
Your Uncle

Letter X

Ignorance

Dear Allen,

Now, I will address our final force—the one that demands the most complexity in our approach and takes the greatest level of intention to resist. Like the other forces, **ignorance** often works in tandem with **victimization**, **isolation**, and **fear**, ensuring that people remain obedient and unaware of their own potential. The goal of **ignorance**—and those who wield it to accumulate control, power, and wealth—is to keep the population complacent, passive, and blind to their own power, to what's really happening, and to the possibilities that lie ahead. As I mentioned earlier, **ignorance** is a force created either by a lack of knowledge or by misinformation, through either neglect or manipulation. There are many subtypes of **ignorance**, each with its own required methods of cultivation.

Ignorance manifests in many forms: ignorance of one's own value, ignorance of others' value, ignorance of history, and ignorance of current events. Each requires different strategies to cultivate, but all serve the same purpose: to prevent people from recognizing their power and potential. When one is ignorant of their own inherent value, they feel either shame or pride. The former makes it easy to manipulate individuals into compliance and the erosion of boundaries—what holds no value requires no protection. The latter can be manipulated through ego-stroking, reinforcing the illusion of superiority and exploiting the desire to defend that false sense of self-importance.

To fertilize the soil necessary for both shame and pride to take root, we must first foster a general distaste for vulnerability. Shame tells us, "What's inside me is inherently bad," so we hide our innermost selves to sustain that lie. Pride, oddly enough, also thrives on concealment—those who are prideful often fear being exposed. This is why the oscillation between pride and shame is so common. The two are natural partners.

We can also cultivate **ignorance** about the inherent value of others, which manifests as prejudice. This subtype can be exploited to garner support for mass harm and to create divisive rifts in society. The strategies for perpetuating prejudice include separation, dehumanization, and misinformation. The key is to ensure that people never have the opportunity to disprove the lies we've fed them about the groups they hold prejudice against. I will address this in detail in an upcoming letter.

Another crucial form of **ignorance** is ignorance of history. The moment certain histories enter the collective consciousness, the seeds of our undoing are planted. We must control the narratives of the past to ensure that people believe the current systems are the only viable path forward. This is why erasing the histories and customs of populations that existed outside the influence of the forces was so critical—doing so was key to preserving our dominance. By controlling language, histories, myths, and stories, we maintain social cohesion and obedience, ensuring the masses stay aligned with our objectives.

Finally, there is the **ignorance** surrounding current events—this includes not only the harm that is being perpetrated in the present moment but also the resistance against it and the deeper corruption that often lurks just beneath the surface. To sustain this type of ignorance, controlling the flow of information is often crucial. When we can manipulate what people see, hear, and understand, we can keep them blind to the realities of what's happening right now. Distraction also plays a key role, especially when efforts to conceal the truth fail. By flooding the public with irrelevant information, shallow entertainment, or sensationalized news, we divert their attention away from systemic issues, ongoing injustices, and potential paths toward meaningful resistance. These constant diversions keep people unaware of the true extent of the harm being done and close their eyes to the opportunities for change. The longer we can maintain this type of **ignorance**, the easier it is to perpetuate the status quo and prevent any significant efforts to confront and resolve the problems at hand.

Ignorance can only be addressed through education, and each subtype requires a different kind of learning to dismantle it. For instance, educating someone out of prejudice involves helping them meet and recognize the value in the people they've been taught to hate, distrust, or dehumanize. Educating someone out of shame requires fostering vulnerability—allowing them to be fully seen and accepted. Educating someone out of ignorance about current events requires exposing the harm that is truly occurring in the world and demonstrating their power to address it.

The good news for us is that genuine education is slow, hands-on, and demanding, while shortcuts like persuasion offer quicker, more gratifying results. This is where we can exploit human impatience. We can encourage those seeking to address **ignorance** to grow frustrated with the process and resort to persuasion instead. Persuasion, in this context, is an alluring shortcut—it promises immediate change and quick wins, but it ultimately fails to tackle the root causes of **ignorance** or the deeper vulnerabilities that allow misinformation to thrive. While education requires sustained effort and time, persuasion offers only a temporary fix. It might sway someone's opinion in the moment, but it doesn't close the cognitive gaps that make them susceptible to future manipulation. This creates an opportunity for a manipulator with superior rhetorical skills to come along later and easily change that individual's mind again. In contrast, education—though more arduous and less immediate—builds a solid foundation of understanding. This is why we must shift the focus away from genuine education and encourage quicker, less effective methods that preserve **ignorance** over time.

So, how can we cultivate resilience to **ignorance** within ourselves? Building resilience to **ignorance** requires nurturing creativity, curiosity, and critical thinking—qualities that keep the mind alert, engaged, and always questioning. With an active and inquisitive mind, we develop the determination to seek out the truth, challenge falsehoods, and overcome apathy. On the other hand, to weaken resilience to **ignorance** within society, we must pursue the opposite strategy. To maintain control, we need to foster passive minds—minds that engage only as much as is necessary to sustain the system and fuel the markets, but no more. We need just enough creativity, curiosity, and criticism to keep people productive and compliant while ensuring these traits never evolve into the deeper, more disruptive force that challenges the status quo.

Staying awake and keeping the mind active can be exhausting and, at times, even painful. It requires effort and vigilance, constantly looking both outward and inward, and it goes against our natural tendency to seek comfort and ease. However, we must remember that much is at stake. If we allow ourselves to fall into intellectual laziness, we risk losing everything and becoming prey to other manipulators—or to the forces themselves.

More on this soon.

Yours,
Uncle

Letter XI

Prejudice Through Separation

Dear Allen,

I can tell from your letters that some of the strategies I've been teaching you cause discomfort. I understand how you feel—it will take time to grow accustomed to using the forces. When you were younger, you benefited from their application but didn't witness their uglier side. Now, it's time to mature and confront the reality that you've already unknowingly helped create.

Today, we're going to address a particularly unpleasant form of **ignorance** prejudice. It's a pernicious sub-force, and one that I find especially irritating, but the usefulness of a force is not determined by its appeal. Like the other forces, prejudice thrives when combined with others, such as **fear** and **victimization**. Together, they create a divided and disempowered population, ripe for control. A population filled with prejudice is a population divided—and a divided population is a population more easily ruled.

We always want people to have an enemy—someone they can blame for their misfortunes. This enemy can take any form: an individual, a group, an ethnicity, or really anything that can be easily sold. The true enemy of the people is always the forces, but we must ensure they are distracted by a more tangible false enemy. Prejudice plays a critical role in this.

In this letter, I will explain how to effectively cultivate **ignorance** of the 'other'—which can include promoting racism, sexism, and other false beliefs about the inherent worth of individuals or groups. When people fail to recognize the intrinsic value of others, they are far more likely to either actively inflict harm or passively allow injustice to persist. Like all forms of harm, this **ignorance** can be exploited to further our own interests.

If there's one maxim to remember about fostering prejudice, it's this: It's easy to believe lies about those you don't know. That's why separation is essential to creating and sustaining prejudice. Separation prevents people from disproving the lies we tell them. If you think misinformation alone is enough to drive wedges between people with strong connections or social ties, you're likely mistaken—except in extreme circumstances.

The separation I'm referring to is not necessarily physical; it can be emotional or mental as well. As long as people don't see the truth about one another—or recognize the potential in each other—**ignorance** can grow and fester. For example, if there is prejudice against people with a particular sexual proclivity, and those individuals remain silent or hide in shame as a result, the separation persists. It's easy to hold prejudice against those you perceive as deviant when you don't know anyone who fits that category—or aren't aware that you do. When we foster lies, we must always consider how to prevent others from proving us wrong. Whenever we spread myths about a group's incompetence or inferiority, we must block opportunities for them to demonstrate otherwise.

I also feel as though I haven't fully addressed the significance of combining forces. **Ignorance**, when paired with other forces like **victimization**, creates vulnerabilities that make lies more potent. This is one of what I'll call the "recipes"—where combinations of forces enhance their effectiveness. For example, the scapegoat recipe combines **victimization**, separation, and misinformation to place all the blame for harm on a particular group, enabling the promotion of violence or oppression against that group.

Throughout history, we've seen examples of this. When a country or group faces **victimization** (such as humiliation from military defeat or devastation by a plague), they seek someone to blame. This is driven by **victimization**'s need to restore power. To convince people to harm one another and distract them from the true sources of their discontent, we must either convince them that they have no other choice or that the targeted group deserves it. When **victimization** is combined with the right type of separation and propaganda (a type of ignorance), people will rally against the targeted group with little consideration. This narrative must be crafted carefully. In most cases, gaining the consent of the masses to harm "innocent" people takes time, but with the right vulnerabilities, it can feel almost effortless. When **victimization** is framed effectively, it doesn't matter who the target is, as long as it gives the illusion of restoring power.

Another recipe that combines the forces is the mixture of **ignorance** and **fear**. **Fear** and **ignorance** are often intertwined. To gain obedience or reliance, it's effective to paint the object of our **fear** as something other than human—either as a god or a monster. Dehumanization is a critical aspect of prejudice. When we strip people of their humanity, it becomes easier for the masses to justify violence or oppression against them. **Fear**, combined with dehumanization, makes people willing to commit atrocities they would never have considered otherwise. People **fear** monsters, so we must ensure they forget that what they **fear** is, in fact, human.

We can also dehumanize our own secret police and law enforcement, convincing people that they consist of invincible, all-knowing gods. This fosters the belief that resistance is futile, encouraging submission. Dehumanization—whether of the victimized group or those enforcing control—can always be played to our advantage.

I hope this has been helpful to you. While we must not buy into the stereotypes or beliefs that one ethnic group, gender, or tribe is superior to another, we must still sustain and use them.

We must foster these prejudices to maintain control, but we must never fall prey to them ourselves.

Remember, the forces and myths are tools for us to wield, not truths to embrace.

Respectfully,
Your Uncle

Letter XII

Apathy and Entertainment

Dear Allen,

Apathy is so abundant and easily created; even now, I wonder if it is the default state of humanity. It is the ultimate sleep aid. Remember, it's always easier to get someone to do nothing than to inspire them to act. Allow apathy to increase our power before resorting to tools that inspire action or violence. Even though many have now freed themselves from apathy and joined the recent uprising, your ability to cultivate apathy in the rest of the population will prove critical in preventing the movement from gaining significant momentum. In this letter, I'll share what I, and those who came before me, have learned about creating this powerful tool.

Apathy and contentment are some of the greatest weapons against education and some of the most effective tactics for maintaining **ignorance** and submission. To free oneself from apathy, one needs two things: adequate discomfort within the present reality and a belief that a better reality is possible.

Where people are uncomfortable, prevent the growth of hope. And where people are prone to optimism, keep them comfortable enough that they will not be inspired to do the necessary work to change things.

Entertainment and spectacle go a long way in maintaining contentment and keeping people uninvolved. A distracted population is a population easiest to rule. In times of peace, or without any large-scale movements toward violence, contentment becomes key. The formula is simple: provide just enough to stave off desperation, while offering a steady stream of distractions. When people are fed and entertained, their attention shifts away from resistance, leaving them more pliable and easier to govern.

Be cautious with the use of stories and art for entertainment, though. Capturing or enamoring the mind is not enough. We must lull the mind, not awaken it. Sometimes, the right piece, play, or book can stir someone in such a way that they struggle to return to their previous state of contentment. This is particularly dangerous for us. Provocative art must be avoided at all costs. Art should provide answers, not raise questions. An active mind builds resilience to our lies, as I've mentioned before, and we must prevent that.

One of the most effective ways to keep a citizenry entertained and distracted in a mind-numbing way is by engaging them collectively in some form of light barbarity. While the gladiator games are a thing of the past, there are still options in our current era. Collective entertainment—especially when it involves light violence or cruelty—appeals to the primal instincts of the population, distracting them from more pressing matters and priming them to think of some violence as trivial, which we can later use to our advantage.

This is something our forefathers understood well, and I have sought to revive it in more subtle ways during my reign.

With care,
Your Uncle

The Fixed View of Power

Dear Allen,

As disruptions to the status quo continue and citizens around the world arise, I want to remind you that—if history proves correct as a teacher—the forces will endure. Brace for shifts and changes, and do not anchor yourself in the comfort of things remaining as they are. Though rulership may change, the vital myths and energies will persist as long as the manipulators maintain focus. While their followers may view resistance leaders as moral and just, I see the forces lurking in their souls, waiting to tempt them.

In this letter, I want to discuss a crucial collective myth we must encourage the masses to continue accepting: the idea of power as a fixed resource. There are two ways to perceive power, and their relevance depends on one's position in society and personal ambitions.

For us, power is fixed—a scarce resource that must be accumulated at the expense of others. We've built a system where we benefit from the disempowerment of those beneath us. In other words, we amass more than our share only by viewing power, and the resources it brings, as limited. But for the common man, power doesn't have to work this way. For him, power can be a renewable resource, shared without the need to subjugate others. However, it's to our advantage to ensure he never realizes this. He must operate under the same belief we do—that power is finite. This belief ensures conflict and disunity within the lower classes and that any new systems of government replicate the same ills as the old ones.

As long as people believe in the fixed view of power, they will fight to protect their position in the social hierarchy, often acting against their own self-interest. This is a brilliant way to sow division and suppress rebellion. As long as people see their empowerment as dependent on the disempowerment of others—whether above or below them on the social ladder—they will remain blind to the systems we've created for our benefit. In other words, they will protect the very rules and structures that harm them and benefit us, as long as they continue to believe in the fixed view of power and are not at the very bottom of the ladder.

They believe the worst position imaginable is at the bottom, but in reality, the worst position is their unwavering adherence to this illusion—the myth they cling to so desperately. This is the power of stratification. We don't need everyone to buy into it, just the majority. And we'll stoke even more **fear** of downward mobility and the threat of powerlessness for those who buy into it the most, so that all their mental energy is spent on pointless defense. Keep them fighting the wrong enemy. This myth of power also interplays perfectly with prejudice.

When we operate within the fixed view of power, it can be difficult to imagine anything different. The idea of equality with those who've been oppressed can be terrifying because we cannot envision a world where power is truly shared—where we're not fighting over a limited resource. This is why so many people are terrified by these ideas. Because if those who have been subjugated adopt the same mentality they've been forced to endure...they're in trouble.

For those who don't require the subjugation of others to meet their needs, power can be a renewable resource. The ladder only exists as long as we believe in it, but we must always keep this truth hidden. If revolution demands that power change hands on the global stage, we must ensure that even if the most oppressed rise to the top, they don't abandon the ladder altogether. The endless defense of their position, the subjugation of others, and the violence needed to sustain it will preserve the forces, allowing us to continue our manipulation.

Until next time,
Your Uncle

Letter XIV

The Importance of Reflection

Dear Allen,

I must address my absence at the recent family gathering, as well as explain why I continue to send letters from my seaside villa rather than from my primary residence in the city. I've been ill—nothing to be overly concerned about, just a lingering ache in my muscles that refuses to let up. I had hoped that some time away would improve things, but I haven't seen any changes yet. Rising each morning is growing increasingly tiresome. I don't say this to worry you, just to inform you in case there are lapses in my future responses.

As it stands now, my attention is all yours. Perhaps this is a blessing. If I were in the city, overwhelmed by my usual affairs and responsibilities, I likely wouldn't have the time for the kind of contemplation required to write these letters to you.

This reminds me that contemplation is essential for us; we cannot live effectively without it.

Self-reflection is critical for those of us who seek to wield power without being consumed by it. Whatever aids this pursuit—whether retreats, walks in the woods, or periods of solitude—should be prioritized. Self-reflection illuminates our emerging vulnerabilities and shows us how to strengthen our defenses in response. We must remain vigilant of these vulnerabilities, for the forces are always waiting to seep in.

We must not fear what we find within ourselves. Vulnerability is a tool for strengthening our defenses against the forces, for it is only when we acknowledge our weaknesses that we can protect ourselves from being overtaken. Often, the barrier to this kind of constructive solitude is a deep shame—the fear that, when we truly look at ourselves, we may find the reflection unsettling. The honesty required to strip ourselves bare and not look away is something few can summon. At this point, the idealized self dissolves, and all that remains is what we have truly cultivated in our short lives.

As I write to you from my seaside villa, I find myself reflecting not just on my physical state, but on the deeper shifts within. The strength I once took pride in has faded, and I now look upon a form that feels foreign. There is a coldness to my body, an unfamiliarity I cannot fully grasp. And yet, I remain here with myself until I can understand the weak and ugly parts.

I do not feel victimized, for I have what I'm meant to have, and I have lost what I was meant to lose. I do not feel afraid, for whatever lies ahead will surely be a great adventure. I do not feel that misinformation clouds my mind, my sense of self, or my approach to the world. But I do feel alone these days. I share this with you to remind you that **isolation** is one of the most insidious forces. Acknowledging it is the first step toward breaking its hold—though, I confess, I am a bit too weary to seek out connection.

But back to contemplation: Remember that resilience to the forces is rooted in self-knowledge and self-accountability. When we know ourselves—and the extent of our responsibilities—the forces lose their persuasiveness. Now that you understand these energies and how they operate, observe their presence everywhere—not only to learn how to harness them but also to learn how to avoid them. You'll hear the voices of the forces in phrases like:

I had no other choice. I had to hurt him.

Taking a few bucks won't hurt him. He has loads, and I have nothing.

Why did it have to happen to me? Why did I lose everything?

People are obnoxious and simply not worth my time.

I'm not hateful, but I find that tribe to just be pretty innately incompetent.

Watch for these. Stay vigilant of the conversations within your mind, and confront the forces whenever they appear.

I will return to rest and anxiously await your response.

Yours,
Uncle

Letter XV

The Purpose of Education

Dear Allen,

I know my letters have been brief as of late, but today, I find myself both inspired and energized to discuss education. Amid the current turmoil, education may feel like a dull subject, but I assure you, the insights enclosed in this letter will be crucial for your strategies when calm eventually returns to these lands and young minds require proper shaping. The right type of education is vital to maintaining your position in the world. This may seem counterintuitive. After all, if we aim for an ignorant, passive population, why would we bother to educate them?

There are two reasons why I'm instructing you on this. First, the people will likely be educated regardless, so it is critical that we take control of this process before anyone else does. Second, your goal isn't to rule a population mired in nothing but poverty. Our vision should not be for a stagnant world where the forces thrive but nothing is achieved. Your goal should be to foster a thriving economy—one where you can benefit from the fruits of such achievements. If nothing is created, nothing can be accumulated—and accumulation is the goal. A population without skills or purpose, offering no value and pursuing no innovation, doesn't bode well for our pursuits. A population with no purpose isn't worth manipulating in the first place.

Education is a vital tool, not only for shaping minds that contribute to the economy but also for reinforcing the subtle myths that keep the forces thriving. While we need creativity, curiosity, and criticism, these traits must always be kept within boundaries that prevent them from unraveling our control. The focus of education should be on the right skills and knowledge to foster a flourishing market, while subtly undermining trust in the individual, the body, and the self. Here are a few principles to keep in mind, especially as reform often follows tumultuous and disruptive eras.

We must strive for elegant subtlety. As the country's operations become perceived in the favor of the people, the education system cannot lean too heavily toward overt control or rigid classrooms. Such an approach might work in more authoritarian regimes, but not where we wish to assert our influence more subtly. In a society driven by commerce, self-expression and individualism are valued—this plays to our advantage, as it creates the illusion that we truly care about each child, emphasizing their unique talents and abilities. It is essential that educators also buy into this illusion. We must make self-actualization appear attainable within our institutions so that our precious students don't seek it in the wrong places, through dangerous ideologies or subversive literature. Of course, the true goal is not for them to follow their purpose but rather to secure their place in our carefully constructed arena.

One of the keys to education is fostering an active mind, but not one that's overactive. Minds that question too deeply or think too creatively can reveal the cracks in the systems we've built. A careful balance is necessary—enough engagement to fuel productivity, but not so much as to spark a revolution.

There are three core features of an active mind. First, creativity—the desire to create something that has never existed before. As is often said, nothing is truly original. Therefore, we must ensure that the source of creativity is one we can control, so that whatever emerges from it aligns with the world we wish to shape. We must encourage the creation of new things, but not things that are too revolutionary or too advanced. If they stray too far from the practical, they may birth a new reality that we are unprepared to handle.

The second feature of an active mind is criticism, which allows us to evaluate what is and identify what is wrong with it. This is essential for innovation, engineering, and invention. Creativity without criticism is simply idle art with no practical purpose for us. We must nurture minds that can analyze effectively—minds capable of deconstructing ideas and understanding what is truly important. However, we must halt the development of this skill when criticism begins to expand into larger existential questions—questions about life, society, or belief systems. When one applies the same critical eye to his life, religion, or relationship with the world as he does to a machine, he may begin to wake up. That dissatisfaction, paired with the hope for a better world, can spark a dangerous awakening. If such a critical and imaginative individual manages to inspire others, then we may face a significant threat.

The third feature is curiosity. It has such an innocent sound to it, doesn't it? The child, full of questions, eager to understand everything. Such a trait is endearing for a time. But when curiosity begins to probe the unanswerable questions within the context of the world we've built, it becomes a source of irritation and frustration. Curiosity must be nurtured, but only in ways that lead to the knowledge we deem valuable—of the knowable universe, of things that contribute to progress within the system. When curiosity shifts to the fundamental "why" and "how" questions—when it begins to challenge the very foundation of the world we've created—it becomes dangerous.

We need all of these—creativity, criticism, curiosity—in moderate, controlled amounts, channeled in safe directions. We neither want inactive minds, nor overly active minds. Overactive curiosity will lead them to truths that expose the forces—or our manipulation of them. Overactive criticism will enable them to see through our lies. And overactive creativity will allow them to imagine and build a world that threatens our pursuits.

Additionally, when crafting curricula around literature and history, be mindful of their influence on the collective imagination. The way we shape the past directly impacts how the masses imagine their future. History must be framed in such a way that limits the potential for revolutionary thought. Present every war as a struggle between good and bad, so people will empathize with one side and demonize the other. Portray movements as flawless and untarnished, setting the expectation that future progress will follow the same trajectory. Erase the histories of those times or regions where our influence didn't reign so they forget what life could look like without our control. Obliterate memories of methods that neutralized the forces, of more just judicial practices, of paths to deeper connection, and of those who cultivated true courage.

I do not concern myself or you with pedagogy or theory; only these principles matter. How you choose to apply them is entirely up to you.

To the future we control,
Your Uncle

Letter XVI

Information Overload

Dear Allen,

The truth is becoming harder to conceal, and the influence of your chosen leaders is weakening as a result. What you need now is not to prevent the truth's exposure—it is too late for that. Your new objective is to make the truth so difficult to grasp, so tangled in conflicting yet persuasive narratives, that it becomes impossible to comprehend. In this letter, I will share the subtle art of using information overload to cultivate apathy toward truth.

Hiding the truth through censorship is obvious, but burying it in a barrage of too much information is subtle. Just as I prefer fostering reliance rather than obedience when working with **fear**, I prefer the more delicate and subtle manipulation when it comes to **ignorance**. This will be particularly important as these dramatic changes unfold and the era of brute force comes to an end. Instead of burning books, print more of them. Instead of shutting down publications, discredit the accurate ones. Print an abundance of nonsense to drown out the sense. Only censor when absolutely necessary, as a last resort. When there is too much to know and too many perspectives to take into account, we make the pursuit of truth seem exhausting. Most people will either construct their own narratives from the fragments we provide or simply decide it's too difficult, too complicated, and not worth the effort to form an informed opinion.

When there is too much information, people experience a kind of mental fatigue. The mind grows tired of sorting through contradictions, and individuals become more willing to accept surface-level explanations, even when those explanations serve our interests. If we want to conceal our own violence, we must report heavily on the violence of others—whether that of a neighbor or of our carefully chosen scapegoat. If we wish to hide our own corruption, we must highlight or fabricate the corruption of another, or sow doubt about the accuracy of the reports. When the true horrors we support begin to surface, publish a string of differing (yet well-articulated) opinions so that the idea of a single, undeniable truth feels elusive. Make sure there are so many "sides" to a given story that the reader or audience simply gives up.

Discrediting accurate information must be done with care. There is no need to outright claim it is false; simply introduce enough doubt, enough alternative narratives, so that the truth becomes just another perspective among many. Confusion and complexity often serve as shortcuts to apathy. When you hide something, you increase its value, prompting people to seek it out and expose it. That which is protected promotes curiosity. But truths buried under layers of complexity and disinformation are rarely seen as worth uncovering.

Additionally, I've observed that your information teams excel at spreading news of atrocities that people are incapable of confronting. This teaches the mind to feel helpless in the face of such horrors, which primes the citizenry to remain silent when you or your leaders overstep. Continue highlighting the ills and tragedies of the world in a way that emphasizes how little the reader can do about them. The more information we push that offers no actionable insights, the more we condition the public to believe that nothing they do truly matters. When people lose faith in their ability to effect change, hope withers and apathy takes hold. Once they accept that meaningful change is impossible, they become easier to manipulate and less of a threat to our objectives. Justice, so glaringly absent in society, is framed as an unattainable ideal. To fight for it is portrayed as swimming upstream—exhausting, futile, and ultimately pointless. Encourage acceptance of the status quo; after all, the effort required to change the world should be seen as simply not worth it.

Remember, balance is key. Too much control or overt censorship will backfire, sparking curiosity. But overwhelm the people with excessive information, and they will sink deeper into apathy.

In trust,
Your Uncle

Discontinuity of Self

Dear Allen,

Everyone has a desire to maintain consistency in their thoughts, beliefs, and actions—but when the forces are present and persistent, we make that consistency nearly impossible. Through their nature of gradual disempowerment, the forces encourage us to act outside of our own values and outside of what we truly desire for our future. They cause misalignment. The more misaligned we become, the less aware we are of our own truth.

Fear, **victimization**, **ignorance**, and **isolation** all work to gradually erode one's sense of self. Each force pulls the individual away from their values and weakens their consistency, making them more malleable to our control. We've turned almost all of our citizens into hypocrites, giving us a lasting and important foothold. By eroding their sense of self, their confidence in their abilities, and their belief in their own goodness, we've launched an assault on their innate desire for congruency. We've convinced the man who claims to love justice to look the other way as his dissident neighbor disappears at the hands of our secret police. We've encouraged the hero to retreat when it mattered most, when **fear** took hold. We've transformed the woman of charity into one of greed by making her feel victimized.

The more misaligned people become, the easier they are to manipulate. Hypocrisy creates a mental fog, blinding them to their own contradictions. This weakens their resolve and makes them easier to control. The further one strays from their own integrity, the more vulnerable they are to our influence. To be a person of your word is always challenging; our task is to make it nearly impossible.

This is why I repeatedly stress the importance of being honest with yourself. Do not delude yourself into thinking you are a "good person" or an altruist—because you will never live up to that ideal. As manipulators, we must live without the illusion of moral purity. Self-honesty is our armor. If consistency is key and your role is accumulation, then you must make peace with your greed. You must listen to it and trust it to guide you, and never pretend it isn't there. If you do, the dissonance will inevitably crack your armor and weaken you. Just as we do to our citizens, this dissonance will inhibit your ability to create and sustain momentum. The moment you deceive yourself into believing you're better than the masses is the moment you expose yourself to the same weaknesses we exploit in them. The weight of that dissonance will pull you down, I assure you—as I believe it did your father, who, rather than creating peace by accepting himself, launched a war that was never resolved, not even in his death. He could not reconcile who he was inherently with what he wanted to achieve in the world or what he wanted for you, his only child.

Your mother had a part to play in this. Though her influence was brief, it left a significant impression on him. Her idealism, her vision for what the world could be for you and your children, became your father's focus. And once anyone realized the path he had chosen, it was too late—there was no turning back. So, I want you to be cautious about who you allow into your inner circle and whose opinions you choose to listen to.

Surround yourself with those who accept your true nature but are not afraid to challenge your strategy. People who reject your desires or nature will lead you astray, just as they did with your father. To maintain consistency and avoid the trap of self-delusion, you must choose your confidants wisely. Ensure that those around you challenge your decisions without rejecting who you are—because if they do, you'll either begin to question your nature or align yourself with their vision.

Dissonance is the seed of your destruction. The more it grows, the more it will pull you down. Master yourself, or you will unravel, just as your father did.

Until next time,
Your Uncle

Letter XVIII

Discrediting the Cause

Dear Allen,

The resistance movements are gaining momentum, more than I even anticipated. We may be on the cusp of a change that ripples around the globe, altering the structures of domination. Your chosen leader is likely distressed (and rightly so), but there are still strategies he has yet to employ. Before we get into those, I want to remind you once again: do not cling to a leader longer than it serves you. Replacement may not be necessary at this point, but you must continue preparing for the moment when it is.

When efforts to funnel resistance into either passivity or violence fail, your next line of defense will be to discredit and undermine the cause or causes. These tactics kill hope, cripple efforts, and inspire inaction of the masses. If executed correctly, your leader can lure an awakened population back into apathy and lull it back to sleep. Fortunately for you—and more so for your leader—this is usually an easy task. It erodes the belief that a better future or a change of leadership is tangible, or that such a shift will improve the lives of the majority. The optimism of the movement gradually begins to look more and more like naivety.

Discrediting the movement's leaders, exposing scandals, and fostering infighting will not only make those involved less effective and impassioned but will also dampen recruitment. This will easily encourage passivity in those who might have otherwise joined, especially those looking for any excuse to avoid action. In the face of change that demands hard work, most people are secretly hoping for a way out—and it's your job to provide it. The pain of persistence is something most are ill-equipped to handle, particularly those who have grown accustomed to comfort.

Our efforts should focus on instilling this mindset in those considering resistance: *There's nothing I can really do to challenge this unfairness. The only movement that stands a chance is riddled with corruption, ineffectiveness, moral ambiguity, and endless infighting.* Make the movement so flawed that those who value order and their public image will refuse to be associated with it.

There are many ways to accomplish this. First, you can spread rumors about the movement's leaders. These can be based on truth if you're able to uncover dirt, but they can also be fabricated when necessary. Find something real that has been hidden in shame and expose it. If you discover a weakness or sinful tendency that could compromise the leader, craft a trap they can't resist. And if both of these approaches fail, you can always invent something. But it must be done with precision. The rumor should surface subtly, not erupt suddenly. Ensure there are months of whispers before the fabricated scandal is revealed. There is an art to this, and I can connect you with the right craftsman should the need arise.

Desperation is a powerful state, and as hope begins to fade, even the most principled leaders will grasp at the forces—**victimization**, **isolation**, **fear**, and **ignorance**—like lifelines. Yet these supposed lifelines only drag them further into our control. In their desperation, they often make compromises from which they can never recover, including forming ill-advised partnerships. These alliances, often with powerful individuals they see as essential to achieving their goals, ultimately corrupt their movements from within, injecting them once again with the forces.

Even the most steadfast activists, in moments of weakness, can fall into these traps. Prolonged **victimization** is especially effective at nurturing this desperation, followed closely by **fear**. Your role is to gently guide them to this breaking point, ensuring they come to believe there is no other option.

In this state of despair, they are more likely to fall for the classic fallacy: "The enemy of my enemy is my friend." Often, this "friend" is a hidden ally of the very forces they oppose. When leaders align with the wrong supporters, they undermine their cause entirely. Once this happens, seize the opportunity to expose their missteps, reducing them to their failures and dismantling everything they've built. This is the cycle—your success lies in patience, waiting for them to step into the trap. Always be ready to exploit moments when their hope is nearly extinguished.

To speed things up, you can also deploy your own people to inspire violence or drum up new scandals from the inside. This is where you'll employ what I call the "little helpers" tactic. There are a few ways to execute this. First, your little helper can join the movement and begin poisoning the minds of its leaders or followers with the forces. This works particularly well in moments of desperation or impatience. Tell them their efforts aren't working—even when they are. Convince them they need to accept another approach, and that the only reasonable options are passivity or violence—both of which, I remind you, can be used to our advantage.

The second, simpler use of our "little helpers" is to send a few people to act as the "bad egg" at one of their demonstrations. It might start as a peaceful protest, but all it takes is one brutish, violent actor to escalate things, and that's all anyone will remember. Violence is always compelling. The majority won't suspect a thing. People already perceive revolutionaries as suspect—dirty, emotional, or untrustworthy—and they'll readily accept whatever narrative we feed them. These little helpers are a timeless tactic, still effective in shaping public opinion, even if those within the movement see right through them.

Lastly, one of the most effective ways to destabilize a movement is by sowing distrust, hatred, and competition among its members while ensuring that potential allies from other movements with similar goals are seen as adversaries.

Division is your greatest ally. If executed correctly, this tactic can dismantle even the most cohesive resistance from within.

Much of this work must be done covertly. Movements striving for change often fall victim to their own ideals, particularly their pursuit of moral purity. Use this to your advantage. Amplify minor disagreements into major disputes, stoking debates over strategy, ethics, or leadership to fracture their unity. Highlight perceived hypocrisies or inconsistencies in their principles, turning their own values into weapons against them. This tactic is particularly effective because it preys on the very foundations of movements—their reliance on collective action and mutual support. By corrupting their paths to unity, you ensure they waste energy battling one another rather than focusing on the larger enemy.

The seaside is growing warm again. If you're interested in paying me a visit, I welcome you. As I write this, the waves gently lap against the shore, and the shouts of gulls fill the air. Surely, the city is growing wearisome, and all this messy business must be exhausting. If you seek a reprieve, consider a holiday here.

Until then,
Your Uncle

The Power of the Individual

Dear Allen,

This letter will be brief, as the growing ache of recent weeks has drained me. However, on this national holiday, which commemorates the life and death of such a great historical figure, I am reminded of an important type of ignorance that can serve us well—particularly as these resistance movements gain traction. We must always seek to foster **ignorance** regarding the power of the individual, encouraging either an overestimation or an underestimation of the impact one person can have.

When recounting the history of great movements—especially those that helped establish the political systems we now uphold—we should always highlight (or, when necessary, fabricate) a few heroes to claim the majority of the credit. Make it appear as though a single individual, with perhaps a touch of assistance, was able to bring about sweeping change through sheer willpower, intelligence, and dedication. The role of the collective, the community, or the countless unacknowledged contributors must always be minimized. Encourage people to pursue an unattainable ideal of heroism, to focus on achieving perfection rather than engaging in the more practical and collaborative forms of organizing. Let them believe that, as long as they embody the perfect, charismatic leader, they alone can change the world.

This approach will likely attract those with the largest egos—individuals who are easier to manipulate and who, in turn, will struggle to gain the trust or followership of others. If our people fail to live up to the impossible standards we set for our "saints"—if they lack the time, energy, or courage to pursue change with such relentless fervor—they will come to believe that they are powerless to effect any real transformation. And when they reach this conclusion, they will give up.

We must, however, also be careful with this myth of the individual hero. You must see to it that your chosen leader does not become too much of a symbol. Leaders who rise too high, who become the embodiment of the cause itself, are always at risk of falling just as far. They are ultimately made to be sacrificed. Remember, the world is quick to build monuments—and just as quick to tear them down. The higher the pedestal, the harder the fall.

Successful movements are never dependent on one individual alone, though the people often forget this. The leader may be the voice, but the masses are the lungs. The leader can be replaced—but only if the movement remains intact. If the people believe the movement is embodied in one person alone, then when that leader falls (and they all do), everything they've built falls with them. History is littered with the bodies of heroes who forgot this simple truth, left to hang for their followers to mourn, only to be quickly forgotten as the next figurehead rises in their place.

We should also make the ordinary individual feel that they can never make a meaningful difference in the world. While this may seem to contradict what I've said before, remember that the goal is to push people to the extremes. We must prevent them from recognizing the power of the individual within the collective and instead foster the belief that one voice alone, in the dark, simply does not matter. Let them forget that movements succeed precisely because of the accumulation of such voices.

You can again see the importance of our storytelling, our holidays, and our education system. Every small detail plays a crucial role, either helping or hindering us. Very few myths and legends exist that are neutral toward the forces.

I encourage you to stay vigilant. The tides of change are ever unpredictable, and the moment a leader rises too high, they are at risk of being toppled. Prepare for the possibility of replacement when it serves your interests.

With care,
Your Uncle

The Empires Are Falling

Dear Allen,

I've just received word from the gallows. I know your chosen leader meant a great deal to you, and I want to express my condolences. Grieve as you will, but keep it brief—your next actions will be of the utmost importance. As the empire we've so carefully propped up over the past two centuries begins to crumble, all is not lost. This has happened before, and we have always survived these disillusions of power. I assure you, we will survive this one too.

A new world will inevitably rise from these ashes, as it has countless times throughout history. But remember this: your place is not with those who fall. Do not rush to aid those from the old system. Just as your leader now hangs in the gallows, others will follow. Let them. Their time is over. Empires, like men, are meant to die.

We have grown comfortable with the networks and systems that sustained us and lined our pockets, but now is the time to relinquish our grip. In the coming years, your only task is to maintain the forces and protect what we have built. Everything else must fall away.

Your first role is to foster and nurture the forces. While you may not be able to fully harness them in the coming months, ensure they persist. Even as leaders fall, the forces of **victimization**, **fear**, **isolation**, and **ignorance** must continue to simmer beneath the surface. Stir the pot quietly. Guide leaders—even the most well-intentioned ones—toward the forces. They will be drawn to them in their desperation.

Your second role is to retreat into the shadows. Secrecy is your greatest weapon now. Stay out of sight as the old system collapses. Soon enough, the calm will return, and with it, new myths, new institutions, and new ways to harness control. This is not the end—it is merely the beginning of a new phase for us. What I've taught you remains relevant, even in the face of revolution, because the forces are eternal.

This revolution will create fertile soil for new ways of thinking and new systems of control. Be nimble. Adapt quickly. You will need to find ways of injecting the forces into these new systems, just as we've done before. The most dangerous moment is the void between regimes—when power is shifting and no one is yet secure in their position. This is where we thrive, quietly shaping the new world while others fight over the remnants of the old one. You'll use our resources to shape the world once again in our image.

Do not be disheartened by the change, for it will offer even greater opportunities for control than you can imagine.

With enough patience and subtlety, you may find that we can manipulate this new world far more effectively than we ever did the old.

Remember, this is the nature of empires: they rise, and they fall, but the manipulators—the quiet hands behind the curtain—endure. The ache in my body has not relented, and while it pains me to admit it, I fear my time is growing short. But I have prepared you well. I pass the torch to you now— use it wisely. In time, you will see that our rule will continue. We may lose leaders and systems, but we will never lose the forces.

Yours in confidence,
Your Uncle

Letter XXI

True Freedom

Allen,

You've applied my teachings well. I can see your strategic manipulations already taking root among the new leaders and systems. The way they speak, imagine the future, and handle opposition reveals, in subtle ways, that the forces are once again growing. This should bring me satisfaction. And yet, as I write this, I find none. Instead, something gnaws at me, something I can no longer ignore.

In recent weeks, I've been reflecting on my conversations with the dissident woman—the one we tried so hard to break yet ultimately failed to subdue. I've replayed those moments over and over in my mind, and only recently did I grasp what had been eluding me. She wasn't merely resilient against **fear**; she possessed an incredible resistance to *all* the forces. And that realization has led me to another—a revelation that undermines the very foundation of what I've believed my entire life.

She seemed to understand the forces instinctively, even without naming them. In many ways, her understanding surpassed mine—despite all my years of study and the accumulated wisdom passed down through generations of our family. What disturbed me most wasn't just her ability to see through the lies—though she did so with unnerving ease. Nor was it her unyielding dignity in the face of unimaginable humiliation, steadfastly refusing to succumb to **victimization**. No, what unsettled me most was her resilience to the force I've explored the least in my letters: **isolation**.

In solitary confinement—where most would break—she radiated a sense of belonging stronger than anything I've ever encountered, even among the tightest-knit communities. This is the part I've been fixated on. I know I could never possess such unshakable strength, and I envy her for it. She claimed her only driving force was love but that never made sense to me. Surely, one could cultivate such resilience without love?

Yesterday, a truth dawned on me, and I fear it may shatter everything I have ever known. Her resilience to **isolation** has shown me just how profoundly I've misunderstood this force. And this realization answers a question that has burned within me since my grandfather first introduced me to the forces: *Can we, as manipulators, truly wield the forces and remain free from them?* Her life—and the essence of her resilience—answers that question with a resounding *no*.

Isolation is not merely the absence of connection with others. It is the forgetting of our inherent connection to something greater than ourselves. **Isolation**, in all its forms, is an illusion—a lie we have inhabited for far too long. It is the denial of belonging—not just to other people, but to the very fabric of existence. And once someone remembers their place in that greater whole, no force can isolate them.

But what is that larger thing to which we are all connected? Perhaps common humanity, but there is something more. The dissident woman didn't seem religious, at least not in the traditional sense. I even asked one of her guards to confirm that she had no religious practices. Yet she carried with her a profound devotion—an unwavering sense of purpose. Could it be that her resilience stemmed from a commitment to something greater than herself? She served not her ego or needs, but a cause—justice, freedom, or perhaps even love itself—that gave her life meaning in ways that accumulation and control never could. It wasn't just belonging to a larger whole, but the pursuit of a purpose beyond personal gain that shielded her from the forces.

It seems that the pursuit of purpose itself fosters resilience—not only against **isolation** but against all the forces. When we are connected to something greater than ourselves, we can still be hurt, but we are not victimized. We may feel alone, but we are not isolated. We may experience fear, but we are not consumed by it. And even in the absence of information, we remain tethered to a deeper truth.

Herein lies my greatest disquiet: our pursuit of accumulation—the pursuit of control—does not connect us to something larger. On the contrary, it severs us from the whole, from the very source that could set us free. This hunger, this insatiable desire to manipulate and amass, is not a purpose. It is a denial of belonging. A denial of the other. A denial of *ourselves*. It is the path to **isolation** and a thief of our freedom.

In harming others, we harm ourselves and submit to the forces' control. That is the truth I have spent my life denying, but I can no longer turn away from it. The woman's resilience has exposed the roadblock that we, manipulators, have been blind to for generations: as long as we seek to accumulate, we remain enslaved. **Isolation** tightens its grip on us even as we remain unaware of it. We are not free, my dear nephew.

So now I must ask you, is it worth it? I urge you to reflect deeply. I have accumulated more wealth and power than I could have ever imagined, yet I remain vulnerable to the very forces I sought to control. Has it been enough? Does it satisfy?

It is for you to decide. I will not command you to follow in my footsteps, nor will I claim that your father's path was the correct one. But I feel an obligation to share this truth with you, even if it contradicts everything I've taught you thus far. I do not wish for you to become another version of me without fully understanding the cost.

Yours,
Uncle

Epilogue

Dear reader,

Thank you for sitting with these letters. I hope this book serves as both an introduction to the forces that perpetuate harm and an invitation to the ongoing, collective work of eradicating them. These pages were not created in **isolation**. They are built upon and inspired by the labor, wisdom, and insights of authors, activists, Indigenous thinkers, artists, theologians, former combatants, and countless others who have witnessed these forces at work and creatively resisted them in the pursuit of a freer world.

I hope these letters inspire you to engage in the essential work of addressing harm at its root, cultivating resilience against the forces, and rendering manipulators irrelevant. I also hope they instill in you the unwavering conviction that protecting and asserting the dignity and humanity of all people in our pursuit of change is not only right but necessary. Together, we hold immense power to transform our communities and create a better, more beautiful world for everyone.

When I set out to write a book, my initial intent was to focus primarily on solutions. But I quickly realized that the exploration of transformative strategies is best undertaken collectively—through deep connection, shared successes, and honest reflections on failures. I'm far more interested in a tapestry of world-changing ideas drawn from people actively engaged in the pursuit of liberation than a single narrative authored by me. These letters, I hope, will become a living work—one piece in a larger fabric of shared knowledge that challenges, inspires, and evolves with us.

In this journey toward collective liberation, we all have a role to play. If you are already engaged in this work, thank you. If you are still searching for your role, keep going. We need your vision, your creativity, your courage. And if you have stories to share—about what's working, what you're learning, or what needs more support or amplification—I want to hear them. Let us grow this community of changemakers, rooted in the collective wisdom and experiences of those who dare to imagine and build something entirely new.

Thank you for being here, for wrestling with these ideas, and for standing alongside me and so many others in this effort. Together, we can illuminate the current reality and forge new paths forward.

Let's keep building.

Share Your Story:

Join the AllFree Movement:

AllFree is a movement dedicated to inspiring, informing, and connecting individuals and communities around the world in the pursuit of collective liberation.

Dedication

This book is dedicated to **our children**—those no longer here, whom we've failed to protect, and those who continue to remind us of the world we're striving to build.
They deserve(d) everything.

Acknowledgments

I want to thank my family for their unwavering support. To my mother—who nurtured in me a deep curiosity and a passion for justice—thank you for encouraging me to explore the world, for releasing me to seek my own path, and for creating the space to process these ideas aloud over countless conversations.

To the former combatants who courageously shared their stories with me—your pasts, traumas, fears, and motivations for taking up arms—I am forever grateful. Your perspectives have profoundly shaped my understanding of this work.

Finally, to every person I've encountered along this journey who is courageously addressing the root causes of harm and creating lasting, positive change in their communities—and to my partners in the pursuit of collective liberation—you are the reason this book exists. The hope that your work inspires fuels my belief in the possibility of a better world. I couldn't have written this without you.

About the Author

Hannah Claire Smith is a writer, educator, and advocate for justice, known for her insightful explorations of systemic violence and oppression and the transformative initiatives designed to dismantle them. Her first major project, *Why We Fight*, was a groundbreaking portrait and interview series that evolved into an immersive gallery experience, offering profound insights into the personal motivations behind taking up arms. This project laid the foundation for the framework that inspired *How to Control the World*.

Hannah's commitment to uncovering and addressing the root causes of harm has taken her around the globe—from Lebanon to Colombia, Iraq to Northern Ireland—where she has gathered stories and perspectives from those at the heart of conflict. Outside of her work, she finds inspiration in nature hikes, the music of Erik Satie, and meaningful conversations with changemakers worldwide.

Follow her on TikTok and Instagram: @hannah.claire.smith